Late Fire, Late Snow

ROBERT FRANCIS

Late
Fire
Late
Snow

New and Uncollected Poems

THE UNIVERSITY OF MASSACHUSETTS PRESS

LC 92–7991
ISBN 0–87023–813–2 (cloth); 0–87023–814–0 (paper)

Library of Congress Cataloging-in-Publication Data

Francis, Robert, 1901–1987
Late fire, late snow : new and uncollected poems / Robert Francis.
 p. cm.
ISBN 0–87023–813–2 (alk. paper).—ISBN 0–87023–814–0 (pbk. : alk. paper)
I. Title.
PS3511.R237L37   1992
811'.52—dc20   92–7991   CIP

British Library Cataloguing in Publication data are available.

Printed in the United States of America

Some of the poems in this collection first appeared in *The Christian Science Monitor, Field, Forum, The Hollins Critic, Liaison, The Lyric, The Massachusetts Review, New-England Galaxy, New Letters, The New York Times, The Painted Bride Quarterly, Poetry, The Virginia Quarterly Review,* and *Voices.* "The Pumpkin Man," "Gray Squirrel," "The Long Shower," "Alma Natura," "Cadence," "The Gypsy Moth Man," and "Old Poet" were originally printed in *Butter Hill,* a chapbook published in 1984 by Paul W. Carman.

Contents

Contents

one

Surf
like a row of washerwomen
kneeling at their eternal suds as if
they could never never get it clean enough.

Salt-white the sail,
white the talisman shell—
what else has the sea been doing all these years?

What else has the sea been saying to itself,
the polysyllabic?

The older a man
the harder the labor of keeping clean
and the more unpardonable his uncleanness.

Less than the sea
is needed to wash the hands
but is there ever more than enough to wash the mind?

Over and over under the gulls' inspection bloom
the white morning-glories.

Silence
can wash as well as water,
silence and distance and the flow of birds.

And still
as if there were all
the time in the world they kneel
at the long scrubbingboard, white daybreak to white moon.

Divers

Where the white water-lilies float upon black water
Boys sleek and dripping as the stems of water-lilies
Run and dive shallow from their tipping raft, their aim
Not to touch bottom when their white heels disappear.

But give them a deep pool paved with white sand and pebbles
Or cove of some blue mineral lake and watch them plunge
Straight down until, breathless, until a muskrat head
Bobs up and then a hand clutching the trophy sand.

Flowers of Death

Chris strolling by the Majorcan sea
Had picked blue flowers for his hair
Or to tuck behind an ear

When an old man's baggy form drew near:
"They're periwinkles, flowers of death.
 Throw them down, young man. Beware!"

But why, I want to ask Robert Graves,
Since death is everywhere—
In the blue sea, in the blue air

Should not the flowers of death be worn
Appropriately in a young man's hair—
As spell against death, or as death dare?

Shells

The shell-producer needing something
analogous to a skeletal structure
bent exclusively on self-protection
a safe home in the sea

By chance models its artifact
on a Greek amphora, a spiral
stairway, a Chinese dragon rampant
or a fan eternally spread

And having lived its life dies
leaving behind in pure abandon
as if it no longer mattered
amphora, stairway, dragon, fan.

Somehow

Somehow over so many years I was fed
not on food but on the aroma
of food.

Fragrance that whets the appetite half-
satisfied the appetite it whetted
somehow.

And when at last I had a few indubitable
meals, I thought them feast
and banquet

Though actually they were only sumptuous crumbs,
so much to revel in yet still
so little.

And now again, these dwindling years
I am reduced to fragrance
only.

November Willows

My slow eyes
Only today have
Seen November willows

Willows with all
Their sweeping pendant
Leaves still golden

After all other
Beech, birch, maple
Golds have gone

Only today after
These many years
Of half-seeing

Suddenly in mist
Rain or clearing
This November gold.

Appraisal

I who have made a virtue and a skill
Of compromise, defending it as a mean,
Though less than golden, among various goods,
A resolution of conflicting goods,
A goal and measure of maturity,
Find myself guilty in this young man's eyes
Looking at me out of a prison sentence.
I do not ask why he is there. I know.
The asking is all his. The man condemned
Condemns the man too safe, the man too wise.
Even the straight clean parting of his hair
Crosses my most felicitous compromise.
He looks at me asking me do I dare.
Looking at him I think that I could dare.

Loan Exhibit

Sunday a rainy
Sunday afternoon say

After Sunday dinner
Something to take

The children to
Indoors and quiet

Prince Radziwill (Polish)
His jousting harness

Polished and glinting
He fought valiantly

Against Russia (note)
And was wounded

At the siege
Of Polotsk (date)

Behind the armor
The appropriate tapestry

Also of course
A few weapons

Designed to pierce
Armor or shatter

Sword and battle
Ax also polished

Safely in glass
Cases or boldly

Outside for instance
The 12-foot lance

The little Dutch
Cannon 17th century

Also Lord Jeffery
Amherst in armor

(Reynolds) so tasteful
Everything so spotless

No speck of
Dust of course

Above all no
Hint of blood.

The Great Wind

Instead of war came wind. Not news of wind
Three thousand miles away but wind itself
East from the sea, heavy and dark with rain.

No man will ever count the trees that fell.

We were expecting war. That was the month.
Each day we thought the headlines would be war.
But we were wrong. We were a little early.

How clean, how beautiful the great wind was.

Late Cricket

The celibate cricket
Concealed and alone
In his hermit cell
Deep in a thicket
Of grass by a stone
In a field on a hill
In numb November
When breath blows chill
And earth turns somber
Still rings his bell
"All's well, all's well"
Till white bird December
Has feathered and flown.

Midsummer

Twelve white cattle on the crest,
Milk-white against the chicory skies,
Six gazing south, six gazing west
With the blue distance in their eyes.
Twelve white cattle standing still.
Why should they move? There are no flies
To tease them on this wind-washed hill.
Twelve white cattle utterly at rest.
Why should they graze? They are past grazing.
They have cropped the grass, they have had their fill.
Now they stand gazing, they stand gazing.
Only the tall redtop about their knees
And the white clouds above the hill
Move in the softly moving breeze.
The cattle move not, they are still.

Curious how the old
Are not called old
Instead are called older
Older being if not
Actually younger than old
Somehow softer. The old
Are also often called
Not elder but elderly
As when we speak
Of an elderly gentleman.
In spite of this
The old are inescapably
Old and growing inescapably
Older day by day
Like you, like me.

Himalaya

Great age
Great mountain

From hard
To always

Harder to
Almost beyond

The limit
To lift

One step
More if

Only one
More step

Few win
The summit

But age
Great age

Never never
Finally wins

Bravura

a rooster
never before
a rooster at my door

fugitive
by God
and free

arterial red
his wattles
arterial blood

his jerking comb
like Hector
taunting to battle

tail feathers black
and up
each feather a sickle

tiptoe he pranced
tiptoe strutted
tiptoe danced

and kept flexing
each yellow claw
like a race horse

pawing to go
race horse or
male dancer

and as he pranced
he eyed
my little house

as if it were
the Trojan Horse
I swear he did

never before
at my own door
such omen

what did he mean
ay what did he mean
adrenalin

wake up old man
wake up and dance
you're not yet dead

courage
color
ardor

perfect silence
my God
if he had crowed!

two

I

That profile where
Have I seen
Before? On what
Old Greek coin?

II

Head bowing deeply
Over the instrument.
Youth with guitar?
Angel with lute?

III

Himself an instrument
Now tuned now
Out of tune
But music music.

In Character

What a happy
What a heavenly
Way to go—

Wafted away to
The other world
On wings of song.

Ah yes, yes
The Boston Symphony
In Symphony Hall.

During what music
The news item
Did not disclose.

Bach or Brahms
Or any other
Of the heavenly.

But I suspect
An unheavenly modern
Composer it was

Who killed her.
No matter now.
Enough to know

A Boston woman
Died while listening
To the BSO.

The Mockery of Great Music

in a world in which there is no harmony
of nations, no cunning counterpoint
no loving orchestration.

I'm tired of being mocked, sublimely mocked.
Less music or no music at all I cry
but a little peace.

If I were God, your orthodox God, demanding
legal compensation, substitution
a divine swap

I'd sacrifice it all as in the Atonement
so that the death of music became
the birth of peace.

Bach would be gone and Brahms and all the heavenly
choristers, but in their place
ah, in their place!

The Listener

Watching the listener I forgot to listen.
I saw the music that the listener heard.
I saw a music that was not for hearing.

The young head long ago bronze in the light
(A light within the bronze) brooding yet lifted—
Where is the listener now and to what music?

T'ang Poems

These words are cool as old tombstones
In a lost graveyard under pines;
Brief as chiseled epitaphs
Telling of a time long dead.

The Pumpkin Man

All summer long and all day long he sits
And fills a chair outside his shanty door.
And now he swats a fly and now he spits
And now is unassertive as before.

In contour, color, general disposition
He comes as near as human nature can
To pumpkinhood—a pumpkin's range, ambition,
Outlook on life. Briefly, a pumpkin man.

Here from my house he looks superbly fed
Though when he eats and what I cannot tell.
If sometime after dark he goes to bed
And sleeps, I think he must sleep very well.

But all day long and summer long he sits
And contemplates poor busy-body me
The way a toad might overtax its wits
Watching the antics of a nervous bee.

Gray Squirrel

Flighty as birds, fluid as fishes
He flies, he floats through boughs, he flashes,
Almost before he starts he finishes.
As rain runs silver down a tree
He runs straight up quicksilverly.
He whizzes, he somersaults, he whirls
Like a plurality of squirrels
    Then suddenly sits
    With all his wits.
How could I catch him, how can I match him
Except with a fast eye and my best wishes?

And Took the Danger Dancing

That hot-cool-headed and light-footed boy
Who ran skipping over the topmost bank
Of oars of his father's trireme in my schooldays
Has been skipping in and out of my mind
For thirty years. Did he do it on a dare,
Or just for the wild and beautiful heck of it?
Whyever it was, he made the slashing blades
That could so easily have been his death
His drums and cymbals, and took the danger dancing.

Chimáphila

A girl named
Chimáphila the Greek
For winter-loving

Might well flower
Into a star
Skates or skis

Ice or snow
A starring girl
In any wise

She would be
Herself a flower
Like Rose like

Violet like Lily
Listen her mother's
Calling her *Chimáphila*?

The Far-Northern Birch

The white birch born so far in the white north,
Bowed by so high a wind, so deep a cold
That it lies down while young into a vine
Invites no white regret or grief of mine.

The fate that fells it is half-fostering fate.
Leaves that will never fling a fountain jet
Still flow and flutter as a rivulet.
Yielding, it still does not capitulate.

White tree of so precarious a birth,
White tree, green tree, grown bowed before grown old,
To you my greetings with no tinge of grief
So long as spring begets the leaf, the leaf.

White Against Evergreen

To hold the breath as these boughs hold the snow.
Then quietly to let breath come and go

And still not take a further step or stir—
Snow-enchanted like each snow-charmed fir

Before the flutter of the first snowbird
Out of the sky is heard or overheard.

Only to stand and see them standing there
Before the sun is their discoverer.

And then to close the eyelids having seen
Absolute white against earth's evergreen.

If Heaven At All

Heaven before I die if heaven at all.
A heavenly now however brief, a few
Celestial days or hours I can distil
From the eternal turbulent flow of things.

Autumn with (heaven knows) what heaps of gold
Around me and above. Instead of harps
A golden silence often as I can have it.
Vision far more than merely visionary.

And as for angels, more beautiful, more real
The young, swift-footed, strong, and visible,
Blond or dark or auburn like the leaves.
Yes, heaven before I die if heaven at all.

In autumn he is all autumn
His hair a field of off-gold grain
Leaf, flower, autumnal fruit.

But after, long after autumn
The world oblivious in white
He is autumnal still.

Late Fire Late Snow

White age supposedly retired
Above ground or below
When suddenly a flare
Of superannuated fire
Fire—or a late late snow
After the snowdrops
After the crocuses
How the great flakes plaster
The whole blooming earth
As if to say I'll show them
As if to say I'm still above
For another day
Oh it is far more than bluster
Remember Goethe old Goethe
Goethe in love.

three

The Whippoorwill

At first we welcomed them. They were so far away
The mimicking of whippoorwill by whippoorwill
Made the still night more still.

And we amused ourselves by trying to count their calls.
Then they came nearer, halfway from there to here,
Nearer yet not too near.

Suddenly, very close, one bird had found us out
And rang and rang like an unanswered telephone
In a house left alone.

Why wouldn't it go away and be a bird again?
A swarm of fireflies, gold to green, was the only light
Tinting, taunting the night.

I cannot blame the bird for keeping us awake.
We would not have gone to sleep had there been no whippoorwill
And the night never so still.

The Long Shower

Sloshing and sleeking like a waterfall
His hair like moss, it pounds, it pours
On him till having cooled his head,
Invades his mind,
Annulling even the memory of heat,
Yesterday's and the day before's.

In a loud solitude of assaulting drops
He stands, veiled and unveiled,
Dazzling and plain,
To everything beyond his whirlwind world
Oblivious and water-dazed
While one hand gropes to force the furious rain.

Cold, cold, cold, how it comes at him
Like anger, like insult, flat in the face
Or, better, some gusty Greek god's masquerade.
How he lets it come!
And now, gently, a sleeper's trying to swim,
His arms lift to a half-embrace.

Does he think old ocean spouts him endless water?
He backs against the blast,
Slowly, slowly takes on metal, turns
Bronze warrior.
Heat present conquered and heat past—
What is there left to slay, boy, but heat future?

Alma Natura

A humor broad to match the body,
Far too exuberant to be bawdy.

A voice out of the stomach, burly.
Hair wind-blown like a sheaf of barley.

Barefoot. What modern shoe could boot her?
Ah, more than barefoot, more the better.

A bust no bra could hope to capture.
Let Peter Rubens paint the picture.

The Last Least King

Though eagle kings, king eagles, were centuries extinct
He could have been a golden-crowned kinglet
The last, the least.

Instead he chose to chuck the crown, the gold, the glitter
And be a mockingbird (of kingship), a dove of peace.
(Some said a goose.)

He made a point (some said a pose) of being poor
To teach the poor to flower in their poorness
Flower above it.

Kingship when it went out went out with him
Finally without a single fanfare
Like a small candle.

Now some are saying he was less bird than saint
Francesco who turned things holy
Upside down.

Are saying that the last king was in truth
The least of all kings kingly, adding that
Least was best.

Eagle

Strong bird, if we could have your strength without your violence,
Your elm-wide wings, your unfailing flight without your crooked hands
And your hooked beak, if we could have your mountains and your seas
Silent without your scream and the battle cries of all the Caesars,
If high were not aloof, if free were more than unconfined,
Strong bird, you would be stamped on something better than our gold.

The Winged Victory

She of the Louvre, one-time of Samothrace,
She of the windy folds, the exultant wings,
You know her—up the long flight of marble stairs—
What do you say, was it chance, nothing but chance,
That let her keep the wings and took the head?

The attendant there in uniform, ask him.
He's dusted off the wings with his duster-feathers
(That were themselves once wings while the bird lived)
Enough times to know. Go up to him and ask
Discreetly if it was chance, nothing but chance.

De Profundis

I'm wild about the sea
A woman said to me.

I looked at her to see
How wild she looked to me.

As far as I could see
She was calm as calm could be.

Looking far out to sea
She never looked at me.

Where could her wildness be?
I looked but could not see.

The Oxen

Massive, submissive, mute
The yoked oxen stand
Waiting the rod's touch.

So in the Iliad
While the rod rested, so
In the Old Testament

With those benign great eyes
Gazing as they now gaze
At something beyond time.

Cadence

Puckered like an old apple she lies abed,
Saying nothing and hearing nothing said,
Not seeing the birthday flowers by her head
To comfort her. She is not comforted.

The room is warm, too warm, but there is chill
Over her eyes and over her tired will.
Her hair is frost in the valley, snow on the hill.
Night is falling and the wind is still.

Grandfather

Grandfather, after all these years, if you were living
And we could sit and talk as once we used to do,
You'd find me far less wise, though a little more forgiving.
And you? I wouldn't wish for any change in you.
Here you could spend contented and uncounted hours
Beside the window in this high-backed rocking chair,
Now prophesying revolutions, wars or showers,
Now playing uneventful games of solitaire.

The Brass Candlestick

Long ago I touched my father's hand
His father's hand had touched.

I have done what I could, have shined
The dented thin brass candlestick
And burned, now and then, one white candle
Against the thinness of the year, the long
Evening, dimness, solstice, and dusk.

And seen the flame in the still room shiver
As in a ghost of wind, or moveless like
The tear-drop evening star, and with the black
Iron box-snuffers trimmed the charred wick
And in the candle's light have lived and breathed

And still the old man would not come.

The Old Peppermint Ladies

Nobody ever called it a presumption
A white peppermint in church

A white peppermint on a warm sabbath
The peppermint being both warm and cool

But that was long ago, the peppermints
Are gone and all the old peppermint ladies

With their palmleaf fans, their folding fans
I presume so, I presume so

Their Psalms, Proverbs, and Ecclesiastes,
Their folded hands.

"Playing an Old Upright Piano"

FOR JAMES SCHEVILL

The piano is old to be sure
But the player is still older

Yet not too old to play and the piano
Not too old to be played upon.

Piano scarcely shows its age
Either to eye or ear. Not so the player

Though people sometimes tell him
To his face he is looking well.

Upright? In various ways
Both are and always have been.

Old Pump

Old blunderer and old faithful
Should I scold or thank you
Or should I scold and thank you?

Your seemingly unreasonable
Eccentricities, idiosyncrasies,
Your frequent persistent jitters

May not, I admit, be blunders
At all, for you may have
Good reasons beyond my knowing.

But normal or abnormal
Year after year you keep on
Pumping. Therefore my heart-felt thanks.

four

Moveless the Mountain Burns

The road lifts toward the sun
And we who ride
Have more light than we ask.

The road goes up, the sun
Is more than halfway
Down the day, the year.

Moveless the mountain burns
With twofold fire:
Fall and the falling sun.

Nostalgia

Dusk of day and dusk
Of year and a bonfire
Blazing at the street's edge
Under the great sugar maples
More brilliant than any autumn
Flower and far more fragrant
The blue smoke lifting like
Incense from an old altar
Then fading to white ashes
Edged with gold. How innocent
This sweet pollution long ago.

Nursery Song

The moon, the moon is Peeping Tom
At every window in the town,
And half the shades are up for him
And half the shades are down.

Dark windows in the lee of light
He reaches all of them in time,
For Tom is out for all the night
And Tom knows how to climb.

Manifesto of the Simple

We are the dim-witted, the weak-witted
Your dunces and your dumbbells.
We don't know enough to do much harm.

The bright boys, the white-haired boys
Make the big bombs, the big bangs. We couldn't
Make even a little Molotov cocktail.

The bright boys, the white-haired boys
Make the sky dragons, the sky demons
And the bright boys fly them.

We are the retarded who will never catch up,
The mooncalves, moonrakers, the morons.
Progress is not our business.

Who said Be simple? Jesus.
Who said it again? Saint Francis.
And the Shakers, the beautiful Shakers.

We are Mother Earth's simple ones.
We are Mother Earth's simpletons.
We are Mother Goose's simple simons.

Peace.

A Day's Sport

"Fifty hares and a pigeon on the wing.
    Gentlemen, it's been a good day's sport."
    Meanwhile while he slept
    Another hunter equally adept
    At little game and big game
    Bagged one king.

Who

Who was the general
Who slapped a soldier

In the face? Curious
I should remember this

And forget his other
Feats whatever they were.

But if a general
Can slap a soldier

According to the rules
Of Military Courtesy who

Will slap the general
And perchance has slapped

Him already? God or
Karma or the Erinyes?

Play Ball!

Baseball in spring
Football in fall

Ball that we dance at
Pinball we chance at

Ball we were born on
Ball that keeps turning

Ball we will die on
When life stops burning

Then the big wrecking ball
Will knock down all

Ball in its basket
Star in his casket.

The Gypsy Moth Man

With a grave taciturnity
The Gypsy Moth Man works his way
From month to month and tree to tree
From fall until the first of May.

Softly he goes with his small brush
Daubing the treebark here and there
Where mother moths have packed in plush
The eggs that they have laid with care.

Softly. Yet to each dreamless moth
This dumpy little poking man
Is the great God of Death who doth
All the dark mischief that he can.

"Pure Basketball"

No referee
No sirree

You should hear John tell

A game for pals
A game for buddies

Nobody's mean
Or dreams of cheating

Whenever they sport
In heaven's court

This is the way
The angels play

You should hear John tell

Columbarium

Caged in this heavy Latin word,
Or rather say, dead and interred,
Columba, the iridescent bird

Whose breast in light once loved to burn.
And in this no less heavy urn
For earth and iron to intern

Something that earth should lightly know,
Something for air to lift or blow
Delicately like down, like snow.

The Giver

He gave
His life

Or so
We say

He gave
His death

But now
We know

Here by
His grave

How he
Gave both.

Psalm

And he shall be
Like a tree

Like a tree
By the rivers of water

That bringeth forth
His fruit in his season

His leaf also by the water
Shall not wither

Like a tree
By the rivers of water

He shall be
He shall be.

Old Poet

Once again in spring he comes drifting down
Into the summer-tourist traffic lanes—
Half ghost, half natural phenomenon.

And women from glassed decks observe him pass
(As he moves south and they move faster east)
Through telescope, field glass, or opera glass.

His unprogressive progress makes them stare.
A little cool he seems and sinister.
White, utterly white, his bardic beard and hair.

A wanderer so far from his arctic mist,
Mortal and fated and melting as he must—
The wonder is, the wonder is, how long he will persist.

Paradox

A raspberry often
hides itself even
while publicizing itself.

Red deep red
yes, but half-
concealed in leaves.

What raspberry picker
does not know
the teasing paradox?

The same paradox
that I myself
(forgive me) am.

This first trade edition of *Late Fire, Late Snow* was reproduced by offset lithography from the Fort Juniper fine press edition designed by David Bourbeau and printed by Daniel Keleher. The typeface is Dante, designed by Giovanni Mardersteig in 1947 and here set in Monotype by Michael and Winifred Bixler. The calligraphy is by Suzanne Moore. The frontispiece portrait was photographed in 1980 by Robert Lyons, and the portrait following "Paradox" was photographed in 1979 by Frank Faulkner. Printing and binding by Thomson-Shore, Inc.